City **Signs**

To Deka Enver, "Cheekee Cheekee"

Photographs © 2002 Zoran Milich

Kids Can Press gratefully acknowledges the financial support of the Government of Ontario, through the Ontario Media Development Corporation; the Ontario Arts Council; the Canada Council for the Arts; and the Government of Canada, through the CBF, for our publishing activity.

Published in Canada and the U.S. by Kids Can Press Ltd.
25 Dockside Drive, Toronto, ON M5A 0B5

Kids Can Press is a Corus Entertainment Inc. company

www.kidscanpress.com

Edited by Debbie Rogosin
Designed by Karen Powers

Printed and bound in Tseung Kwan O, NT Hong Kong, China, in 1/2018
by Paramount Printing Co. Ltd.

CM 02 0 9 8 7 6 5 4 3
CM PA 05 20 19 18 17 16 15

Library and Archives Canada Cataloguing in Publication

Milich, Zoran
     City signs

ISBN 978-1-55337-003-1 (bound)   ISBN 978-1-55337-748-1 (pbk.)

1. Signs and signboards — Pictorial works. I. Title.

GT3910.M54 2002   j659.13'42   C2001-902830-X

City Signs

Zoran **Milich**

Kids Can Press

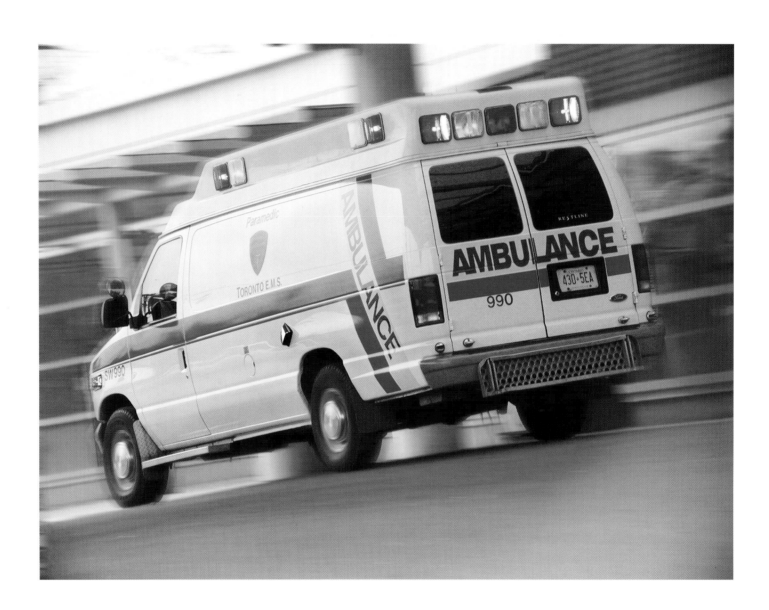

PIZZA
Delive
GOURMET PI
Fornarina(tomato sauce, mushrooms and
Vivace(tomato sauce, garlic, onions and romano)
Vegitariana